JOSIE SMITH IN SPRING

Spring brings surprises for Josie Smith! She finds out that you can plant seeds if you invent a garden; that your mum can make you steal something by accident, and that there's more than one kind of Easter egg.

JOSIE SMITH
IN SPRING

Magdalen Nabb

Illustrations by Karen Donnelly

Galaxy

CHIVERS PRESS
BATH

First published 2000
by
Collins
This Large Print edition published by
Chivers Press
by arrangement with
HarperCollins Publishers
2002

ISBN 0 7540 7802 7

British Library Cataloguing in Publication Data

Nabb, Magdalen, 1947–
  Josie Smith in Spring.—Large print ed.
  1. Smith, Josie (Fictitious character)—Juvenile fiction
  2. Children's stories, English 3. Large type books
  I. Title II. Donnelly, Karen
  823.9'14[J]

ISBN 0-7540-7802-7

Printed and bound in Great Britain by
BOOKCRAFT, Midsomer Norton, Somerset

CONTENTS

JOSIE SMITH AND FRIENDS

Josie Smith

Ginger

Mum

Eileen

Gran

Geoffrey Taylor

Garry Grimes

Jimmy Earnshaw

Rawley Baxter

Rawley's sister

Miss Potts

Mr Scowcroft

Mr Kefford

Mrs Chadwick

Ann Lomax

Tahara

SOW IN EARLY SPRING

'Can I play out?' asked Josie Smith. 'I want to help Mr Scowcroft.'

'It's pouring down,' said Josie's mum. 'Wait till the sun comes out.' She was peeling potatoes and onions for a pie.

Josie Smith knelt at the kitchen window, waiting for the sun to come out. It sunshines when you go to school and on Saturday morning it rains.

Great big clouds, black, grey and white, were going past the chimney tops. The wind was blowing them about and spattering the raindrops

1

sideways on the glass. The back yard looked cold and wet and full of little puddles.

'The sun's coming out!' shouted Josie Smith. A patch of pure blue sky opened out behind the chimneys and all the raindrops glittered.

But before she had pulled one wellington on, the rain was pattering at the window and the day was dark again.

Josie's mum put the potatoes and onions in with the meat and turned the gas up. 'Why don't you go and play at Eileen's?' she said. 'I don't

want you both round here, not today.'

That was because she was making a wedding dress and there were big pieces of cut-out satin, still pinned to the tissue paper pattern, all over the couch and armchairs and even on the carpet in the front room.

Josie Smith put her wellingtons on and her camouflage green anorak and one old brown glove that she found in the pocket. Then she went to the front door and looked out. She saw the cold wind blow Mrs Scowcroft's umbrella inside out as she came up the street with her shopping bag. Josie Smith went to help her but Mrs Scowcroft, struggling to keep hold, said, 'It's no use messing with it. You have to turn into the wind and it'll blow itself right.'

But the wind blew this way and then it blew that way and Mrs Scowcroft turned into it until she was dizzy and her nose was red and wet.

Then the sun came out. Josie Smith smiled and the puddles glittered with the pure pale blue of the sky. Now she could go and help Mr Scowcroft to dig in his allotment.

She ran all the way and got out of breath. The cold wind made her nose red, but it didn't rain.

'Can I come in Mr Scowcroft?' shouted Josie Smith, pushing the gate.

Mr Scowcroft had a pipe between his teeth and a cap on his head and a sack over his shoulders for the rain. Josie Smith wished she'd brought her piece of sack that he'd given  her once to go home in the wet. Mr Scowcroft didn't stop work when it rained. He took no notice of it at all and neither did his hens. They kept on walking stiffly about, looking for worms with their red brown feathers wet and shining. Mr Scowcroft was bending down to put a big square of glass over something.

'What are you doing, Mr Scowcroft?'

'Early lettuce,' he said and sucked on his pipe. No smoke came out of it. He wiped the glass clean with a rag and Josie Smith looked through it as hard as she could but she couldn't see anything.

'I can't see any lettuce, Mr Scowcroft,' she said.

Mr Scowcroft stood up straight and sucked on his pipe. Pah. Pah, pah. Then he took from his big pocket a seed packet with a picture of fresh green lettuce on it. He poked a stick into the empty packet and planted it in the ground behind the glass frame.

'They're lettuce seeds!' said Josie Smith. 'Will real lettuce grow there, just like the ones in Mr Kefford's shop?'

'I've my dahlias to sow yet,' Mr Scowcroft said, 'but I'll keep them inside for a while.'

'Are they pom pom dahlias, Mr Scowcroft?'

'Aye,' Mr Scowcroft said. He always said Aye when he meant Yes. Josie Smith followed him into the shed where there were plant pots all piled up and a workbench with two wooden trays on it amongst a lot of dusty stuff.

'Can I help you, Mr Scowcroft?' Josie Smith said.

Mr Scowcroft pointed at the trays

with his pipe. 'Put a bit of humus in them,' he said, opening a big plastic bag and giving her a green trowel.

Josie Smith dug into the big bag and lifted out a trowelful of soft brown soil. She sniffed its damp smell before letting it fall into the first tray. She worked very hard without talking while Mr Scowcroft mended things, twisting wire with pliers in his big knobbly hands and sucking on his pipe. Pah. Pah, pah. Josie Smith liked the trowel and she liked the soft warm soil that Mr Scowcroft called humus. She liked it so much that she took her glove off and shovelled with her hands for a bit. But when she was filling the second tray she saw something she liked even better. Seed

packets. Lots of seed packets with pictures of beautiful flowers on them. Yellow flowers, orange flowers, pale blue and pink flowers, so fresh and bright that Josie Smith held her breath looking at them.

'I wish I had a packet of seeds . . .' she said, and a lump came in her throat from loving the bright flowers so hard. Then she remembered that they were Mr Scowcroft's seed packets and he might think she was asking for them instead of just wishing. She looked at him but he was busy pulling at a nail with the claw of his hammer and he wasn't noticing her. When he stopped work it was only so he could light his pipe. Pah. Pah, pah. So Josie Smith could carry on wishing and shovelling.

'I wish I had a packet of seeds,' she wished and shovelled.

Then she thought for a bit and started again.

'I wish I had some humus and a trowel so I could wish for a packet of seeds,' she wished and shovelled.

Then she thought for a bit and started again.

'I wish I had a garden so I could wish for some humus and a trowel and then wish for a packet of seeds,' she wished and shovelled.

'Have you done?' Mr Scowcroft said.

'I think so, Mr Scowcroft,' Josie Smith said. 'Is that enough?'

'It'll do,' Mr Scowcroft said.

'What are you going to plant in them?' Josie Smith asked. 'Are you going to plant those?' She pointed at the packet of seeds that she liked best of all, the orange and yellow flowers and fresh round leaves of Nasturtium *(Whirlybird mixed)*.

'Bit of parsley,' Mr Scowcroft said. 'The wife likes a bit of parsley with her fish.'

'My mum does as well,' Josie Smith said.

'I'll give you a few seeds to take home,' Mr Scowcroft said.

'Thank you, Mr Scowcroft. But, Mr Scowcroft, I haven't got any trays or any humus. And I haven't got a trowel . . .'

8

'They'll do well enough outside,' Mr Scowcroft said, and he shook some seeds out of a big packet into a screw of newspaper for her.

'Thank you Mr Scowcroft.' Josie Smith squeezed the screw of newspaper tight and held her breath. If she told Mr Scowcroft she had nowhere to plant the seeds outside either, he might think she didn't want them, and she did. Only, how could she explain that she really wanted seeds in a packet that she could plant on a stick. She looked at the packet of Nasturtium *(Whirlybird mixed)* and held her breath so hard she nearly cried.

Mr Scowcroft sucked on his pipe and blew some little puffs of smoke. 'What's to do with you?' he said. 'You look like you've lost a pound and found sixpence.'

'I haven't got a garden, Mr Scowcroft.'

'Well? You've a back yard, haven't you?'

'Yes.'

'Here.' He gave her what was left of the plastic bag of humus and said, 'Pull

9

a flag up. Mind it's a sunny corner.'

He put the humus bag into a paper carrier bag for her and she put the seeds in their screw of newspaper into her anorak pocket.

And then Mr Scowcroft picked up a packet of flower seeds. Josie Smith's chest went Bam Bam Bam and she held her breath again. Mr Scowcroft opened the packet and poured a few seeds into another screw of paper.

'Antirrhinums,' he said. 'Snap-dragons, like. Put them in your other pocket. Parsley round the edge. A few flowers in the middle for you.' He folded the open edge of the seed packet closed again and he started to put it away.

'Mr Scowcroft, please can I . . . please can . . . please can I look at the picture?'

He showed her the packet. 'See there. Mouths like little dragons. Bite your finger, them will, when they're out.' The flowers were pale yellow and pink and dark red. 'Best be off home. It's coming on to rain.' He didn't tell her to put her hood up like other

10

grown-ups would and when she got outside his gate the wind blew a shower of cold rain in her face. She had to put the carrier bag down so she could put her hood up and pull the strings tight.

'Here!' It was Mr Scowcroft shouting. 'Wait a bit!' Did he want his seeds back? Josie Smith watched him coming towards her in the rain and her chest was going Bam Bam Bam. Sometimes Eileen gave her things and then wanted them back.

'Here,' he said, 'you left one of your gloves.' He held it out and Josie Smith took it, remembering to say Thank you.

'Give me them seeds,' Mr Scowcroft said. 'Not the parsley, the

11

antirrhinums. Can you remember which is which?'

Josie Smith could remember. She pulled them out of her pocket and gave them back to him without saying anything. He took the screw of paper from her and said with his pipe between his teeth, 'You'd best take these. You'll happen want to read the instructions.' And he gave her the rest of the seeds in their beautiful packet.

'Thank you very much, Mr Scowcroft!'

'You can read, can you?'

'Yes, Mr Scowcroft. Mr Scowcroft, I'm best in the class at . . .'

'A sunny corner, now. Think on.' Mr Scowcroft was going away. Pah. Pah, pah.

Josie Smith put her glove on and pushed the seed packet deep into her pocket and set off home with her carrier bag.

Even though it was cold and wet, Josie Smith didn't run. She didn't want to bang the carrier bag about or lose the seeds from her pockets. It rained really hard, cats and dogs and stair rods, but Josie Smith still didn't run. Her anorak got soaking wet and her brown glove got soaking wet and her bare hand got soaking wet. The paper carrier bag was getting wet, too, but Josie Smith wasn't worried because the humus was safe in its polythene bag inside. Even when she popped down a back street for a minute to go through a specially big puddle that she saw there, Josie Smith didn't run and splash in it. She walked back up through it carefully and only swished about just enough to come out with her wellingtons clean and shiny. Then she turned her own corner and struggled in at the back gate and down the big steps into the yard.

'Mum? Mum!'

Nobody answered. Josie Smith wanted to show her mum what Mr Scowcroft had given her so she went into the kitchen.

'Mum? Mum!'

Nobody answered. The sewing machine was silent. The light under the pan was turned off. Josie Smith just had to show her mum what Mr

Scowcroft had given her so she went into the front room. It was dark and sad and the rain was tapping at the window.

'Mum? Mum!'

Nobody answered. It's horrible when you shout for your mum and there's nobody there. In a small voice Josie Smith said, 'Mum . . .' But the dark empty house got darker and emptier.

'Mum!'

The front door banged and Josie's mum was there with a bag of shopping from Mrs Chadwick's across the road.

'What's to do with you?'

'Nothing! Mum, Mr Scowcroft's given me some seeds called Aunty's dragons and some special soil to plant them and I've got to pull a flag up and it's in a sunny corner and, Mum . . .'

'You're wet through! And what have I told you about playing in this front room today?'

'I'm *not* playing! I only want to show you . . . and, Mum, he gave me the packet because I

14

happen want to read the instructions. Mum, *look* at the picture of the flowers!'

To get the seed packet out of her anorak pocket Josie Smith had to put down her paper carrier bag. As it touched the floor the wet paper collapsed and the plastic bag of humus d r o p p e d through it and fell over, spilling rich brown soil all over the

carpet and all over the long white shapes of satin and tissue paper.

Josie's mum went mad. She shouted so hard that Josie Smith couldn't hear what she was saying because her chest was going Bam. Bam Bam louder than her mum's voice. Josie's mum's face went red and Josie Smith's face went hot and then cold. Her mum pulled her out of the front room, dragged the soaking anorak from her and sent her off with a good smack.

'Get upstairs out of my sight! And change those clothes!'

Josie Smith scrambled up the stairs as fast as she could and her legs were shaking. She didn't change her clothes. She grabbed Percy Panda and curled up on the bed with him, trying to warm her wet hands and face on his woolly head. Then she cried hard and loud until her throat was sore and she couldn't cry any more. She lay there holding Percy close. She pulled his big woolly head nearer to her face because now it was hot and smarting with tears and he made her feel better.

She was so upset and frightened that she couldn't even tell Percy what she'd done. She only said, 'I couldn't help it. I didn't mean to. I'm sorry.' She knew how precious and expensive a wedding dress was. Her mum let her just touch

16

the lace with one finger after washing her hands really carefully. Now the lady wouldn't be able to get married and it would be Josie Smith's fault.

'I'm *really* sorry,' she told Percy, and started crying again.

She was too frightened to go down and tell her mum she was sorry, so she waited, crying a bit and sniffing a bit and holding Percy tight and telling him she was sorry instead.

Then her mum shouted, 'Josie! Come down and get your dinner!'

Her mum was still mad. She put a plate of pie in front of Josie Smith. Bang.

'Do you know how much that satin cost? And who's going to pay for it?'

Josie Smith, holding her breath and thinking hard, thought of collecting returnable bottles, helping to sweep Mr Kefford's greengrocer's shop, asking her gran for 10p, saving her Saturday toffees money. She knew she could never pay for the satin that must have cost pounds and pounds. Josie Smith, hungry and miserable, ate her pie very carefully, swallowing hard to get it past the lump in her throat, not spilling any on the tablecloth. The only lump of potato she dropped landed on her kilt and slid down inside her wellington until it stuck, hot and squishy, near her ankle where her sock had got down to. That didn't matter because anything that happened inside her wellingtons was her own secret.

Only when her mum turned away to look at the rain out in the yard did Josie Smith dare look at her face. And then she saw that her mum wasn't mad now. She was nearly crying. She was as upset and frightened as Josie Smith about the lady's wedding dress.

'Go and play out,' was all Josie's mum said after dinner. 'I'm going upstairs to have a lie down.'

Josie Smith put her blue duffle-coat on because her camouflage green anorak was hanging there soaking wet. She found one of her old brown gloves in the pocket and put that on. Then she opened the back door. She saw her bag of humus outside near the gate and then she remembered her seeds. Were they lost? Were they wet? Josie Smith looked behind the back door and her chest went Bam Bam Bam as she felt in the pockets of her anorak. The seeds were safe! She took the screw of newspaper and the coloured packet and put them in her duffle-coat pocket. Then she went outside. It wasn't raining so much now but it was still very cloudy so how could you tell which was a sunny corner? Josie Smith felt something wet and furry tickle her knee.

'Eeeow!'

'Ginger!' Josie Smith bent down to stroke him. She was glad to see him because he was friends with her. 'You didn't get wet like me, did you?' Ginger never got really wet. When it rained he sheltered and when it stopped for a bit he came in. He wanted to go in now. Josie Smith wished he'd stay out and play with her because she felt lonely but Ginger rubbed his face against her hand and lifted his tail up high and then sat down at the back door.

'Eeeow!'

Josie Smith opened the door and let him go in.

Josie Smith stood looking up at the cloudy sky, wondering which was the sunny corner, and then she remembered Ginger. He didn't like getting wet but he did like sleeping in the sun and he always slept in the sun in the corner at the end of Eileen's wall. So that was the sunny corner! Josie Smith went and looked at the corner flag. It was a great big square stone and she didn't know how she was going to manage to pull it up. She felt the edges with her fingers and pulled a bit but it didn't move. It was a bumpy stone and one of the corners was broken and grass grew there in the dirt. Josie Smith went in the coal place where Ginger usually sheltered. There was a lot of stuff in there, covered with dust and cobwebs, and it smelled a bit like Mr Scowcroft's shed but without the hen food smell. Josie Smith found a long iron rod. She didn't know what it was but it was really strong. She pulled it out from all the other junk and a lot of things fell over and dirt and cobwebs fell on Josie Smith but she didn't notice. She took the long iron rod and a big shovel and she started poking and lifting and pulling and heaving and she got the big flag up. Her face was red and she was hot all over and she scraped one hand but she got the flag up. She hoped there'd be some soil underneath it.

'Ugh!' There was some soil. On the soil and on the underneath of the flag were hundreds of the creepiest, crawliest, dark wriggling creatures that Josie Smith had ever seen. She wished she had two gloves. With her face all screwed up and her eyes almost shut, she pushed the flag and leaned it against the wall with its clean side facing her. Then she went in the kitchen to get a fork and spoon because she didn't have a trowel. She  took them off the table because the washing up hadn't been done and there was no point in dirtying clean ones. When she came out again the wriggly things had disappeared below ground, thank goodness. She did a bit of digging. The fork and spoon didn't work so well because when there was a stone they bent and Josie Smith was working hard and fast so she never saw the stones in time. Now she was working she forgot to be upset and frightened. The harder she dug the happier she got because she was doing something really good for her mum now. When she saw the parsley Josie Smith had planted for her

she would cheer up. Josie Smith tipped some humus on to her sunny corner and spread it out and then wondered what to do next. She hadn't seen Mr Scowcroft planting his seeds. When she got to the allotment he'd finished planting lettuces and when she left he hadn't started planting parsley or his pom pom dahlias. Then she remembered about the instructions and took the packet out.

'I'll happen want to read these,' she said to herself. She read them. Josie Smith was good at reading and she could read all the words on the packet, even the long ones. But sometimes, even when you can read all the words you can't understand what they mean.

Sow in early spring in drills six inches apart. Thin out to one strong seedling . . .

What did it mean, *in drills*? Mr Scowcroft hadn't said anything about drills. Josie Smith remembered every word he'd said. It was easy to remember every word Mr Scowcroft said because he didn't say so much. Other grown-ups say hundreds and hundreds of things and then get mad when you forget one of them.

'Pull a flag up.'

'Mind it's a sunny corner.'

'Parsley round the edge. A few flowers in the middle for you.'

'You'll happen want to read the instructions. You can read?'

Josie Smith read every single thing on the seed packet again. She even read *Price includes 17% VAT* and *To be sold by the 31st October* but she still didn't know what to do. If she had to sow the seeds in drills instead of humus she would have to find out what sort of drill. Eileen's dad had a drill and so did Geoffrey Taylor's dad. She didn't know whether Mr Scowcroft had one or not but she was ashamed to go back and ask him what a drill was after she'd told him she was the best in the class at reading.

Josie Smith put the seeds back in her pocket and went out the back gate to go and find out about drills.

'Black and Decker,' Eileen's dad said. 'I don't lend tools. They never come back and if they do they're broken. What d'you want with a drill? Our Eileen plays with dolls. Girls don't want drills.'

'Look,' Mr Taylor said, 'this bit is for

24

drilling holes, this bit's a screwdriver and I've a sanding attachment as well. You can try it if you want. Does your mum want a job doing?'

Josie Smith went home.

In the front room on the dresser there were a lot of books in a line. Sometimes Josie Smith read the titles of them but the print inside was tiny and dull and there were no pictures. There was a big dictionary, too, though. Josie Smith stood at the front room door feeling frightened. Then she went in. The humus had gone from the carpet and there was no stain. All the satin pieces pinned to their tissue paper were on the couch. Josie Smith didn't go near them. Then she remembered that her hands were dirty from digging and she went to wash them in the kitchen before opening the big dictionary. She was still frightened of being in the front room and she was a bit worried about her wellingtons so she took the dictionary out in the yard and sat down on the step below the gate to read it.

It took a bit of time to find 'drill' because she found a lot of funny things on the way like 'Double Dutch' and 'do with' and 'dribs and drabs'. She also found an important thing called 'downy mildew n. 1. a serious plant disease which affects onions, cauliflower and lettuce.' She read that very carefully so she could warn Mr Scowcroft about it. Then she found 'drill'. It was such a small word but it meant hundreds of things and the dictionary was too heavy to hold on her knees for a long time.

Josie Smith got organised. She took her coat off and spread it on the step so she could put the dictionary down without getting it dirty. Then she sat next to it on the wet cold stone and read hard. She read about rotating tools and cylindrical holes and training for parades and the use of weapons and a strict method of teaching and a sea creature that lives on oysters and hitting a ball in a straight line at speed and that was the end. Nothing about seeds at all. Josie Smith was fed up with the dictionary that told her so many things that she didn't want to know. Mr Scowcroft was better than a dictionary but she couldn't ask him so she carried on reading in case she found another funny word. She found another 'drill'. And then another and another and another. And none of them were any help. There was one that told her about a machine for planting seeds in rows, a small furrow in which seeds are sown and a row of seeds planted using a drill. She still didn't know what to do. Eileen's dad wouldn't lend her his drill and she didn't think Geoffrey Taylor's dad would either. He'd want to come to the house and talk to her mum and the parsley was meant to be a surprise. She tried looking up 'furrow'. It took a long time to find because on the way she found her own 'fringe' and Eileen's 'frizzy' tight curls and 'fudge', her favourite toffee, and 'funny bone'.

'Furrow' was a long narrow trench made with a plough. Nobody in Josie Smith's street had a plough. It was also a long deep groove or a wrinkle on

27

your forehead. Josie Smith covered the dictionary with the folds of her coat because it was spitting rain and went back to her sunny corner.

She had decided what to do. She was going to plant her seeds in humus because that was what Mr Scowcroft did and he was better than a dictionary. With her spoon that was bent out of shape she made a furrow all round the edge of the sunny corner for the parsley. Then she made three short furrows in the centre for the Aunty's dragons. To drill the holes for the seeds she used the long iron rod from the coal place. She pushed it into the furrow, down and down and down until it must have been halfway to Australia and then she pulled it out again. She knelt down with her eye to the deep deep hole and dropped one seed into it. The only trouble was that the seeds were as tiny as a full-stop in a story book and a lot of them slipped through her fingers as she went along her furrows. Still, she had enough to put one seed in each deep hole even though she wasted so many along the way.

'And anyway,' she said to herself as she covered all the furrows with humus and patted it down, 'nothing's ever wasted in the garden. Mr Scowcroft said.'

Parsley all round the edge and the flowers in the middle. She'd finished.

'Josie? Josie!' Josie's mum, her face still pink from her sleep, came out into the yard.

'What the . . .' Josie's mum stopped and stared.

'I've made us a garden,' said Josie

Smith. She opened her eyes as wide as she could to stare at her mum and make her listen and understand. 'It's a surprise.' Josie Smith smiled a big smile to cheer her mum up. Inside her head she could see the sunny corner with its frill of bright green parsley and the pink and yellow and dark red flowers in the centre and Ginger sleeping in the warm sunshine on the wall above. She could see her mum picking parsley for her sauce and herself picking some flowers to put in a glass on the table.

But Josie's mum wasn't smiling. Josie's mum's forehead had furrows in it. She couldn't see the things inside Josie's head. Josie Smith, with her smile getting smaller and sadder, saw the things her mum was looking at. Her muddy wellingtons, her dirty face and hands, one of them bleeding. Her wet fringe plastered to her forehead and her filthy clothes covered with cobwebs. Her coat lying on the step in the wet, the bent and dirty spoon and fork, the rusty iron rod and the shovel and the screw of newspaper and the empty seed packet lying in the dirt. The dirt that had spread all over the yard and in at the kitchen door. The sad grey rain falling on it all.

'Oh . . .' whispered Josie Smith. She had to tell her mum about the green frills of parsley and how good it would taste and how bright the flowers on the seed packet were if you picked it up out of the dirt. She had to tell her.

'I've . . . it's . . .' But all of a sudden she was too tired, too cold, too wet and too sad to tell her anything. She felt her face crumple up and a lump come in her throat and tears that rolled and rolled down her face and under her chin because she wanted her mum. She squeezed her eyes shut to stop the tears but she couldn't. She tried to say, 'It's parsley for you' but she could only say, 'I didn't mean to. I'm sorry. I'm sorry, Mum. I only wanted to show you. I didn't mean to spoil the wedding dress.'

She couldn't talk any more because it hurt. She let herself cry and felt her mum get hold of her tight and warm and carry her into the kitchen and sit down with her on her knee, muddy wellingtons and all.

Her mum's voice said, 'It's all right. It's all right. Nothing's happened. Nothing. It's all right.'

And she rocked Josie Smith backwards and forwards on her knee like when she was little. Josie Smith could hear her mum's voice above her head and feel it next to her ear. She started to feel warm and quiet but she still held on tight to her mum and listened.

'It's all right, now. Nothing's happened. Nothing. Stop crying now. You're better.'

'I know I am. Nff. B-but I can't nff stop nff crying. Why can't I stop nff?'

'It's only because you've overtired yourself. We'll sit here until you feel better and then we'll have a nice cup of tea. Here. Blow your nose.'

Josie Smith blew.

'Are you better now?'

Josie Smith held on tight and, with her throat still sore with crying, said, 'I want to tell you about my seeds.'

'Tell me about your seeds, then.'

Josie Smith told her. Then she remembered. 'I have to plant the packet in the ground like Mr Scowcroft!'

Josie's mum gave her a clothes peg and they planted the seed packet together in the rain. Then they had a cup of tea.

'Mum,' said Josie Smith, 'you were nearly crying as well, weren't you? Did you overtire yourself, like me?'

'I think I did,' said Josie's mum. 'The wedding's not till May and I can buy a bit of satin to re-do the bit that got dirty. I was upset because I wanted to finish the work and get paid before Easter so you could have new shoes and we could have a really nice Easter dinner and a big Easter egg for you. You've always wanted an Easter egg with sugar flowers on it like Eileen

33

gets, haven't you?'

'I used to but I don't any more,' said Josie Smith. 'I only like my seeds now and I'd rather wear my wellies than new shoes.'

'I know that,' said Josie's mum. 'So, have I to buy you a packet of seeds for the sunny corner, now, instead of an Easter egg?'

'Can you just buy them?' asked Josie Smith. 'Real seeds . . . in a packet with a picture on the front like Mr Scowcroft's?'

'Of course you can,' said Josie's mum.

'And can we afford it?' asked Josie Smith.

'They'll cost a lot less than an Easter egg,' said Josie's mum.

Josie Smith could hardly believe that something so wonderful as seeds that would grow into real flowers like in a flower shop could cost less than an Easter egg. An Easter egg looks nice in its box but when you get it out it's just chocolate that doesn't grow into anything at all. When you've eaten it it's gone for ever and the empty box is just squashed cardboard.

'I didn't want an Easter egg like Eileen's because it was bigger,' Josie Smith explained to her mum. 'It was because I could have kept the sugar flowers instead of eating them and cut out the flowers on the box. I like Smarties and you can put lipstick on with them but the box is no good for cutting out.'

'So you'd rather have seeds. Why don't we get them now, so perhaps they'll come up for Easter.'

'Now? Today? Don't we have to see? *Right now*?'

'Why not? Your sunny corner's ready, the shops are open and it's even stopped raining. I could do with a breath of air . . . Josie! Your blue coat! It's still outside.'

'I'll get it,' Josie Smith said. She got it while her mum went upstairs to wash her face. The dictionary was clean and dry but Josie Smith didn't want to do any more explaining. Her coat was dry enough on the inside so they set off to the ironmonger's shop where they had packets of seeds on a rack that twirled round and round. Josie Smith twirled it round and round for a long time, enjoying all the coloured packets, but she was only pretending to choose. She knew very well that when she got home she would have in her hand a bright new beautiful packet of Nasturtium *(Whirlybird mixed)*.

EILEEN'S NEW CLOTHES

Josie Smith and Eileen were walking up to school. It was sunshining and the sky was high and windy.

'I'm having a new frock,' Eileen said, 'for Easter, and it's red with white flowers and a real lace collar.'

'I'm having a new frock, as well,' said Josie Smith. She said it with her eyes a bit shut because sometimes her mum sewed her a new frock for a surprise so she might be really getting one.

'You are not,' Eileen said. 'I know you're not because you've got your eyes shut, so you're telling lies.'

'I'm not,' said Josie Smith.

'Oh yes you are!'

'I am not.'

'You just are! And I'm having new shoes and a really big Easter egg with flowers on it so ner-ner-ner.'

They were passing Mr Scowcroft's allotment. The hens were out scratching for worms but Mr Scowcroft was inside his shed. Josie Smith, walking past, could smell his pipe and the hen mash.

'I don't want an Easter egg with flowers,' she said, 'because I'm going to have some real flowers. I've planted them in my garden.'

'You're a liar,' Eileen said. 'You haven't got a garden.'

'Oh yes I have,' said Josie Smith.

'You have . . . not . . . I've never seen it.' She looked at Josie Smith and saw that her eyes were wide open. 'Will you show it me?'

'If you want,' said Josie Smith, 'but you haven't to touch.'

Rawley Baxter went dashing past with the sleeves of his anorak tied round his neck and his arms sticking straight out.

'Der-der-der-der. Der-der-der-der. Der-der-der-der. Der-der-der-der. Batman!'

'Rawley Baxter's daft,' Eileen said.

Rawley Baxter's little sister ran past them, trying to keep up. She was out of breath. Rawley Baxter's little sister was always out of breath because Rawley Baxter said, 'You've got to keep up with me and don't fall because you're Robin.'

But Batman's legs were long and thin and fast at running. Robin was short and fat. So she ran past, as fast as she could and not falling. 'Aher! Aher! Aher!'

'His sister's daft, as well,' said Eileen. 'I'm having a toffee before we go in.'

They stopped at the school gate and Eileen got a tube of wine gums out of her pink anorak pocket.

Miss Potts, the headmistress, said if the caretaker found toffee papers in the playground there would be trouble. So, some people who had toffees ate them outside the gate. Eileen always had toffees. She started peeling the paper off her tube of wine gums. Josie Smith watched her. Eileen put a red one in her mouth and then an orange one and then a green one. The next one was black.

'Can I have one?' asked Josie Smith.

Eileen looked at the tube of wine gums as if she were counting how many there were left.

'You can have *one*,' she said. But when Josie Smith reached out to take it, she said, 'Not that one. I'm having the black one. You can have a yellow one.' Nobody likes the yellow ones. They taste like yellow washing-up liquid. Eileen had to eat three more, the black one and two red ones stuck together, before there was a yellow one to give to Josie Smith. Josie Smith chewed it but she didn't like it.

The whistle blew and they ran in to line up. In the line, Eileen said, 'On Saturday before I go for my new clothes, I'm going to get a tube of wine gums that are all black.'

'So am I,' said Josie Smith, and then their line went in.

School was horrible all morning. They had to do tens and units and Josie Smith had no rubber. Then she had to hear Gary Grimes read and he'd been on Book Two all year and he still couldn't read it.

'Here— is— the— ball—'

'Go on.'

'Look— at— the —'

'*Go on*!'

'Look— at— the—'

'Ball,' said Josie Smith. 'Here is the ball. Look at the ball! Why can't you read ball on this page if you can read it on that one?'

'Let's play dinky cars,' Gary Grimes said.

'We're supposed to be reading,' Josie Smith said.

'Here,' Gary Grimes said, 'you can have the yellow one.' Then he went, 'Vrummm. Vrummm vrummm,' with the red one. The yellow car only had one wheel left. Gary Grimes ripped the page of his book with the red one and they both got in trouble. Josie Smith felt tired and fed up.

When it's a horrible day at school, it's always a horrible dinner as well. It was spam and beans and chips. Spam is always cold and rubbery and tastes of soap. Josie Smith liked baked beans and chips but you can't eat them when they've gone stone cold because Gary Grimes has dropped his dinner on the floor right at the end of the serving hatch and everybody has to wait for it to be cleared up so they don't tread in it.

After dinner they went out to play and Rawley Baxter being Batman knocked Eileen down and she cried.

'Shall I take her in?' Josie Smith asked Mrs Ormerod who was on duty. Josie Smith liked taking people in when they'd fallen. But Mrs Ormerod said, 'Get up, Eileen, and blow your nose. You haven't even scratched yourself. Rawley Baxter! Rawley Baxter, come here!' She blew as hard as she could on her whistle, puffing up her fat cheeks and turning pink.

But Rawley Baxter didn't take any notice. Rawley Baxter never took any notice of anybody. He went on running and his little sister came along, trying to keep up, not falling. Then she fell.

She didn't cry. She wasn't allowed to

cry because she was Robin. She looked frightened and her face went white.

'For goodness sake!' Mrs Ormerod said, bending down to look at her knee. It was bleeding. 'Take her in, somebody, and get that knee washed.'

'I'll take her in, Mrs Ormerod!'

'Can I take her in, Mrs Ormerod?'

'Can I, Mrs Ormerod?'

'Can I?'

All the girls wanted to take Rawley Baxter's little sister in but Mrs Ormerod said, 'Josie Smith, you take her.'

Josie Smith put her arm round Rawley Baxter's little sister, helping her so hard that she made her limp. She whispered, 'You're really brave for not crying. We have to go to the staff room and tell Miss Potts. Come on.'

Rawley Baxter's little sister was frightened of Miss Potts. She went all floppy and heavy and didn't come on so that Josie Smith had to pull her.

Josie Smith knocked at the staff-room door, feeling very important. A teacher opened it just a bit. Josie Smith loved peeping into the staff room. It was a secret place. She could hear the teachers talking and laughing with different voices than they had in the classroom. She saw Miss Potts with a cup of coffee in her lap and her feet up on a chair. Rawley Baxter's little sister's teacher was Mrs Ormerod and she was outside, so the teacher from Class 4, Mr Eccles, came out with the First Aid box and took them to his classroom. He had to wash the scraped knee with cotton wool and water and get some grit out with the tweezers and dry it with some more cotton wool. Rawley Baxter's little sister didn't cry. Her face was still really white. Mr Eccles had long thin hands and tidy nails. Josie Smith liked his classroom. It smelled of varnish and magic markers and there was a giant cutout painting of a dinosaur going right across one wall.

When Rawley Baxter's little sister was ready, Josie Smith put her arm round her and took her back outside.

'You're all right now,' she said. 'Come on.'

She was all right now. They weren't

going near Miss Potts any more so she came on.

At hometime, Josie Smith was told to see Rawley Baxter's little sister home because they lived in the same street. The teachers knew that if she went home with her brother he would make her run and fall again.

'Can I come, as well?' Eileen said.

'If you want,' said Josie Smith, 'but you have to remember to walk slowly because she's only small.'

'I know what!' Eileen said. 'Let's stop at our houses first and put our nurses' uniforms on!'

So Rawley Baxter's little sister sat on Josie Smith's doorstep, holding Josie Smith's doll and sucking a yellow wine gum while Josie Smith and Eileen got changed. Their mums wouldn't let them go out without their coats over their nurses' uniforms. Josie Smith said it was all right because they could do what Rawley Baxter did. They put their coats round their shoulders and tied the sleeves under their chins so that they were nurses' cloaks. Eileen's uniform had a short cloak to it but

Josie Smith said nurses wore long cloaks so they both used their coats. They walked one on each side of Rawley Baxter's little sister with their arms round her. They helped her so much that her feet hardly ever touched the pavement. They had to let her take Josie Smith's doll or else she wouldn't go.

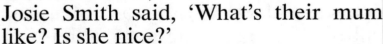

When they got to Rawley Baxter's door, Josie Smith said, 'What's their mum like? Is she nice?'

'I don't know,' said Eileen, 'because she never comes to school, my mum said. And she never goes in Mrs Chadwick's either.'

Rawley Baxter's little sister started pulling backwards like when they had to go and see Miss Potts. She held their hands and took them down to the bottom of the street and round the back. When they got to his back gate, it was open and Rawley Baxter was there in the yard with a big paintbrush in his hand. He wasn't being Batman.

'We've brought your little sister home,' said Josie Smith, 'because Miss Potts said. Have we to take her in?'

But Rawley Baxter's little sister didn't want to be taken in. She ran to the corner of the yard and sat down on an upturned crate near a funny little wooden house.

'Is it a Wendy house?' Eileen asked.

'Don't be daft,' Rawley Baxter said, 'it's a rabbit hutch.'

Rawley Baxter's little sister put the doll on the roof of the hutch. Then she opened a door in the front of it and pulled out a great big grey rabbit with long pink ears and hugged it to her, chattering.

'What's she saying?' Eileen asked.

'Nothing,' Rawley Baxter said. 'She's always like that. Take no notice.' He dipped his big brush into a bucket of thick pink creamy stuff and sloshed it on the wall of the yard.

'What're you doing that for?' Eileen

48

asked.

Rawley Baxter took no notice.

His little sister was still chattering, hugging the big rabbit. Josie Smith had never heard her talk before. Nobody had ever heard her talk. Josie Smith crouched down and said, 'Can I stroke him as well?'

She didn't answer. Josie Smith touched the soft rabbit's fur and the  soft brown hair of Rawley Baxter's little sister who was still chattering. The rabbit was chattering, too, but Josie Smith couldn't understand either of them.

'Here.' Rawley Baxter put a brown paper bag down beside his sister. 'Give him his food.'

Josie Smith watched the rabbit eat pellets from the little sister's plump hand. Then she looked round the yard. She had never been in there before

49

because Rawley Baxter only liked being Batman. As well as the rabbit hutch there was a patch of garden under the kitchen window where two flags had been taken up. Josie Smith wondered if Mr Scowcroft had told them how to do it. She wondered if it was a sunny corner like hers. It was in the shade now. She thought of asking Rawley Baxter what was planted there but he was busy sploshing pink stuff on to the back yard wall. Josie Smith thought she'd ask her mum if they could have pink walls in the yard. It would look nicer with her flowers but perhaps it would cost a lot of money.

Then Eileen said, 'I'm going home for my tea.'

As they went out the gate, Josie Smith looked back. Rawley Baxter was still sploshing pink stuff. His little sister was still chattering. There was a face at the window. A lady's face with red lipstick. She wasn't smiling and Josie Smith was frightened.

'Run!' she said to Eileen. They ran all the way home. Josie Smith's doll was still on the roof of the rabbit hutch.

At bedtime, Josie Smith said, 'Mum? I saw Rawley Baxter's mum and she had red lipstick and she was frightening.'

'Clean your teeth,' said Josie's mum. 'That's not his mum. That's Mr Baxter's second wife. Rawley's mum died very young, poor soul.'

'Why did she die?' asked Josie Smith.

'She was very poorly,' said Josie's mum, 'and Rawley's little sister was only two. She never learned to talk properly.'

'She does talk,' said Josie Smith. 'She talks to a grey rabbit. Mum? Is their dad nice?'

'I think so. But he's never been the same since his first wife died. Just look at that pyjama jacket. There isn't one button left on it. Put your blue and white striped ones on and give those to me.'

'Why does he have to be the same?'
'Who?'

'Rawley Baxter's dad. Mum? Can we paint the yard pink to look nice with my flowers? And, Mum? I've left my doll at Rawley Baxter's.'

'Get to bed. You've got Percy to sleep with. Tomorrow's Saturday and you can get your doll in the afternoon. We're going shopping in the morning with Eileen and her mum, so you've got to be ready early.'

'Are we going to the market? Can I go on the roundabout? Can I have a balloon?'

'We're not going to the market, we're going to a department store.'

'What's a department store? Is there a roundabout?'

'No there isn't. I've got to buy some white satin to finish that wedding frock. It came from there. And I don't want any can-I-having just because Eileen's having all sorts. Now get to sleep.'

Josie Smith didn't get to sleep right away. She had a lot of things to think about like the grey rabbit and Rawley Baxter's poorly mum and the lovely pink stuff to splosh on the walls and her seeds growing down there in their

52

sunny corner in the dark. There were a lot more things as well, but before she could think of them all they started getting muddled up. She was feeding rabbit pellets to her doll in the hutch and Rawley Baxter was painting Eileen's curls pink.

'But it's all right,' whispered Josie Smith to Percy with her eyes closed, 'because Eileen likes pink . . .'

And then she was asleep.

The next morning, when Josie Smith was ready and her mum was nearly ready, Josie Smith said, 'Can I go to Mrs Chadwick's for my Saturday toffees?'

'Suit yourself, but if you spend your money at Mrs Chadwick's don't be asking me for more when we get to the department store.'

'I won't ask for more.'

'Well, why don't you wait and see what there is there? You can go to Mrs Chadwick's any day.'

'I know but I want to go now. Please can I? Eileen's getting a tube of all black fruit gums. She said.'

'And anything Eileen does, you have to do. You'd put your hand in the fire if Eileen did it first.'

Josie Smith dashed into Mrs Chadwick's, all out of breath, clutching her spending money.

'Hello Josie,' Mrs Chadwick said. She was wearing her pink stripy nylon overall and she had earrings and a pink and gold necklace. Mrs Chadwick was very posh. Her house behind the shop had glass doors.

There were loads of things on the counter that Josie Smith liked a lot better than fruit gums. There were liquorice torpedoes, sherbet and spanish, gobstoppers and hundreds and thousands. But Josie Smith still remembered the horrible yellow wine gum and what Eileen had said.

'Please can I have a tube of wine gums,' she said. 'All black ones.'

Mrs Chadwick gave her an ordinary tube of wine gums.

Josie Smith looked at her very hard to make her listen. 'I want one where they're all black.'

'There'll be some black ones in

there. They don't make them all black.'

'Eileen said.'

'Well, I have none.' She looked mad. Mrs Scowcroft came in, ringing the bell.

'Hello, Mrs Scowcroft. How are you keeping?'

Josie Smith ran out.

Afterwards, when they were on the bus, Josie Smith said to Eileen, 'Can I have one of your all black wine gums?'

'I haven't got any. I got liquorice torpedoes only I've left them at home because I'm getting new clothes and I have to keep really clean.'

When they got to the department store Josie Smith didn't like it. It was worse than the indoor market and she hated that. It was crowded and hot and they had to keep hold of their mums' hands all the time so that they wouldn't get lost. People poked their shopping bags in her face and the crowd pushed her one way and her mum pulled her the other. There was a moving staircase that looked a bit frightening but Josie Smith would have liked to have a go on it. They had to go in the

lift with loads of people. Somebody
stood on Josie Smith's foot really hard.

'Ow!'

'Stand still.'

'I am standing still. I can't breathe
because of that
lady's coat.'

'Stop whining
and behave
yourself.'

'Ladies' wear,
children's wear,
lingerie and
hosiery,' said
the liftman.

Eileen and
her mum got out.

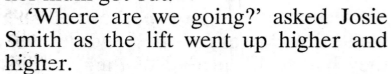

'Where are we going?' asked Josie
Smith as the lift went up higher and
higher.

'Furniture, glassware, tableware,
haberdashery.'

Josie's mum said, 'Come on,' and
pulled Josie Smith out from all the
ladies' coats.

'What's have a dashery?' asked Josie
Smith.

'Keep a hold of my hand,' said

56

Josie's mum.

They went in a big room where it was quieter and there were giant rolls of stuff on long tables. It smelled like the front room at home. Josie's mum let go of Josie Smith's hand and started looking at white satins and asking the prices. She showed a lady in a black frock a piece of satin brought from home. Josie Smith went to look at some white muslin with white velvet specks on it and then at some white net and some soft lace.

The lady in a black frock poked her in the arm and said in a nasty voice, 'Don't you touch anything.'

Josie Smith opened her mouth to say, 'My mum makes wedding dresses all the time and I *never* . . .' Then she remembered that her mum was buying the satin because she'd dirtied it with soil. She stood still and her chest went Bam Bam Bam and she didn't say anything.

'Now where's the lift?' said Josie's mum when she'd finished. 'There it is. Don't get left behind or you'll get lost. You know what you are.'

57

Josie Smith knew. She didn't want to get lost. Anyway, there was nothing to stop and look at, only pots and pans and knives and glasses. Then towels and sheets. Then radios and televisions. Then striped umbrellas and deck chairs.

Then Josie Smith stopped. She saw plant pots, trowels, forks and spades. And then she saw a watering can. It was smaller than the grey one that Mr Scowcroft had, just as if it were made for children. It wasn't a toy though because it wasn't plastic and silly. It was bright red and metal with a brass handle on the side and a bar across the top, and a shiny brass cone at the end of its spout with holes for the water to come out. Josie Smith had never seen a watering can like that except in picture books. Mary Mary Quite Contrary had one just the same. It was on a little stage next to some big plastic plants and a little green shed and a striped chair. All the other people who were looking at things picked them up and touched. Nobody said 'Don't touch.' Josie Smith picked up the bright red beautiful watering can, holding her breath because it was so shiny and new. There was no price on it but she knew, anyway, that she couldn't have it. She just wanted to feel how heavy it was and 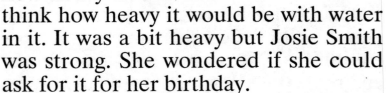 think how heavy it would be with water in it. It was a bit heavy but Josie Smith was strong. She wondered if she could ask for it for her birthday.

'Josie? Josie! What did I tell you?'

'I just . . .'

'The lift! It's arrived. Come *on*!' Josie's mum grabbed her hand and ran with her to the lift. Inside, Josie Smith was squashed again so she couldn't breathe. She pulled at her mum's coat.

'Mum, we've got to go back.'

'Don't pester.'

'But, mum, we've got to. I've got to . . .'

'Now, see! Oh, will you look at your face!' Josie's mum pulled Josie Smith out from between the two big people and got a handkerchief out. She wet it a bit with spit and started rubbing at Josie's nose.

'How you can get dirty without so much as touching anything I'll never know. Keep still!'

Josie Smith hated having her face cleaned like that. It hurt and she didn't like the smell of lipsticky spit. She tried to get her face away and to pull the watering can up from between all the people who were squashing her but she couldn't. The watering can stuck against the leg of a lady who said, 'Mind what you're doing!' Then she gave Josie's mum a nasty look. 'She's laddered my stocking!'

Josie's mum yanked her out of the lift on the Ladies' and children's wear floor and said, without looking at her, 'This is the last time I take you anywhere. Showing me up like that. Now, I'll not tell you again to keep hold of my hand. So, if you get lost like you did at the market, don't come running to me.'

How can you come running to your mum if you're lost? Josie Smith didn't say anything. She held on tight to her mum's hand that was pulling her along and to the watering can that was trailing behind. They'd have to take it back after.

It was easy to find Eileen and Eileen's mum. Eileen was screaming and stamping her feet in a rage. She was hanging on to a clothes rack and wouldn't let go. The lady in a black frock who was serving them looked mad.

'Eileen! For heaven's sake,' said Eileen's mum. She was trying to get Eileen's fingers off the clothes rack but Eileen's fingers gripped so tight they turned white and she screamed so loud that her face was dark red.

'What's to do with her?' asked Josie's mum.

'She doesn't like her new coat,' said

Eileen's mum. 'I've bought her that red and white flowered frock and that red coat to go over it but she wants a pink coat.'

'The pink's very nice, too,' said the lady in black, holding her hands over her ears.

'Ma-ya-ya-yaagh! Ma-ya-ya-yaagh! Maya-ya-yagh!' screamed Eileen. Her screams wobbled in time with her stamping feet.

'The pink coat won't look nice with your red and white frock, Eileen,' said Eileen's mum. 'Look in this mirror and see how nice the red one is.'

Eileen squeezed her fingers tighter round the rack, stamped her feet harder on the carpet and screamed and screamed and screamed.

'And you've got a pink coat already,' said Eileen's mum.

Eileen squeezed tighter, stamped harder and screamed louder.

Everybody was looking at Eileen.

'Would you like her to try the pink one, madam?' asked the lady in black. She looked really fed up. The grown-ups all started talking at once about what to do. Josie Smith didn't care what they did because she was too worried about the watering can. She looked at Eileen. Eileen was still screaming but, now that the grown-ups weren't looking at her, it wasn't real screaming. She was just making a noise and she was looking at the grown-ups talking and waiting to start up properly again when then looked at her. Then she saw Josie Smith and her pretend screaming face looked like it did when she said, 'I'm having loads of new things and you're not.' Then she saw the watering can.

'Maa-ya-ya-yaagh! I wanta wa-ya-ya-yagh can! Ma-ya-ya-yagh!'

Nobody except Josie Smith noticed that she was screaming about something different now. They were putting the clothes Eileen had come in into a carrier bag. The only way to get her out of a shop when she was screaming was to pick her up and carry

63

her. Josie Smith didn't know how they were going to manage that without Eileen's dad.

'Stay there with her while I go and pay,' said Eileen's mum. Josie Smith stayed and the grownups went to pay. As soon as they were out of sight Eileen stopped screaming. She let go of the clothes rack and grabbed at the watering can.

'You can't have it,' Josie Smith said, 'because it's not paid for.'

'My mum can pay for it,' Eileen said and grabbed again.

'You haven't got anything to water,' said Josie Smith.

'I don't care,' said Eileen. 'I don't want to water anything, I want to carry it with my pink coat on and look like Mary Mary.'

'It's the same colour as the red coat and, anyway, you can only carry it back up to the top floor. That's where it lives near some plastic plants. If you keep the red coat you can carry it.'

'All right, then, but I'm carrying it all the way and we have to go on the escalator not in the lift, then I can carry it for longer.'

The grown-ups came back.

'Where's she got that from?' said Eileen's mum.

'It belongs on the top floor,' Josie Smith explained. Nobody listened.

'She didn't have it before,' said Eileen's mum. 'How did she get it here?'

'Josie Smith carried it for me but now I'm carrying it and we have to go on the escalator!'

Josie's mum looked down and said, 'You were carrying it for her?'

'I *was* carrying it,' Josie Smith said, 'but . . .'

Nobody was listening again. They were arranging to meet on the ground floor near the door where the umbrellas were. Eileen's mum was furious because she had to take Eileen up to the top floor. When they had set off towards the escalator, Josie's mum said, 'How ever did you stop her screaming? Nobody else can except you. I'll tell you what! When we get downstairs, let's get ourselves a sample squirt of perfume while we're waiting.'

'What's a sample squirt?' asked Josie Smith. 'And Mum? Can we go on the escalator too, because I get squashed in the lift?'

On the escalator, Josie Smith held her mum's hand because she was a bit worried about getting squashed flat along with the stairs and disappearing like they did into the slot at the bottom.

As they went down, Josie's mum said, 'I've just about had enough of Eileen for today. I don't know why you put up with her.'

'Because she's my best friend,' said Josie Smith. 'And, anyway, if she hadn't taken the watering can back, we'd have had to take it because I was looking at it and . . .'

'Josie! You didn't pinch that watering can upstairs?'

'No,' said Josie Smith, 'I was just . . .'

'What did I tell you about touching?'

'It was all right to touch the watering can. All the grown-ups were touching.'

'And you're not a grown-up.'

'I tried to put it down,' said Josie Smith, 'but you made me get in the lift. You weren't listening.'

'Just look at all the trouble you've caused by not doing as you're told. You made Eileen . . . and now Eileen and her mum . . .'

'What?' said Josie Smith.

'Never mind,' said Josie's mum. 'Let's try some perfume.'

When Eileen and her mum came down, Eileen was still carrying the red watering can.

'I made my mum pay for it,' she said, 'or else I'd start screaming again for the pink coat. But you've got to let me carry it all the way home on the bus.'

'All right,' said Josie Smith, 'but what did you make your mum buy it for if you haven't got anything to water?'

'Because I wanted to carry it,' Eileen said. 'And I made her buy it for you because you're my best friend and I can make my mum buy anything I feel like. Your mum never buys anything.'

'But I thought you wanted the pink coat?'

'I've got a pink coat,' said Eileen. 'This one's only nice for carrying the watering can. I can get rid of it afterwards, easy.'

On Sunday morning, Eileen came out to play in the new red coat.

'We've got to go to Rawley Baxter's first,' said Josie Smith, 'because I left my doll.'

'I know you did,' said Eileen, 'and I've got two pounds.'

'Well?'

'Well! Two wells make a river. You jump in and make it bigger.'

They skipped off down the back till they came to Rawley Baxter's gate. Rawley Baxter and Rawley Baxter's little sister were cleaning out the rabbit hutch.

'I've come for my doll,' said Josie

Smith.

Rawley Baxter's little sister took Josie Smith's hand and made her go in the shed. Then she showed her the doll. Rawley Baxter's little sister had made a sort of bed for Josie Smith's doll in an old wooden crate with newspaper pillows and sheets and a brightly coloured magazine picture for a cover.

'Aw!' said Josie Smith, 'that was really nice of you. You didn't leave her out in the dark.'

Rawley Baxter's little sister picked the doll up very carefully and gave it back to Josie Smith.

When they came out of the shed, Rawley Baxter and Eileen were standing together, waiting. Eileen whispered something in Rawley

Baxter's ear and then she said, 'Go on.'

Rawley Baxter didn't move. Eileen said to Josie Smith, 'Try my new red coat on. You can wear it to walk home, if you want, but don't let my mum see you.'

Josie Smith liked the new red coat because it was the colour of her watering can. She gave her doll to Rawley Baxter's sister to hold and put the red coat on.

'Turn round,' Eileen said to her, 'and let's see how it looks from the back.'

Josie Smith, in the new red coat, turned round.

'Go on,' she heard Eileen say. Then she felt something on her back. Splosh!

She turned round to see what was happening and Rawley Baxter, with his big brush loaded with pale pink paint, came at her. Splash! Splosh! The new red coat was pink.

Josie Smith stood there, too scared to move. Rawley Baxter said, 'She gave me two pounds.' Eileen ran away.

'Eileen!' screamed Josie Smith, grabbing her own coat and running after her. 'Eileen! Wait for me!'

Eileen ran faster than Josie Smith had ever seen her run and went in at her own front door. Slam!

Josie Smith stood there in the pink coat with her chest going Bam Bam Bam. She was going to get blamed. Eileen had made her put the coat on while it was painted so that she'd get the blame. Josie Smith pulled the coat off and put her own coat on.

That made her feel better but the wet pink coat lying on Eileen's doorstep made her cry with fear. She ran in at her own front door.

'Mum!'

'What's to do with you? I thought I told you to play out . . . and don't come in this front room while this wedding frock's here.' Josie's mum didn't stop sewing and she didn't look up. She changed the spool on her sewing machine and said, 'Well? What are you crying about?'

'Mum, Eileen's painted her new red coat pink.' Josie's mum stopped sewing.

'She's what?'

'She's painted her new red coat pink.'

'She hasn't!'

'She has and she's going to blame me. She made me try it on and then . . . and then I felt all this paint sloshing on it and now it's pink and her mum will shout at me.'

'Are you making this up?'

'No.'

'So where did Eileen get pink paint from?'

Josie Smith thought about Rawley Baxter. When he was being Batman he was just Batman. But now she thought about him in the yard with his little sister and the grey rabbit and the frightening face at the window. She didn't say anything.

'Well?' said Josie's mum, waiting for an answer.

Two wells make a river. You jump in

and make it bigger. Josie Smith didn't say anything.

'Are you sure you're not making this up?'

Josie Smith shook her head and whispered, 'It's outside on Eileen's doorstep.'

Josie's mum stopped sewing. She went with Josie Smith to the front door and opened it. They both peered round at Eileen's doorstep. There was nothing there.

Josie's mum looked hard at Josie Smith. She saw how white and frightened she was and she saw the tears on her cheeks. Josie Smith never cried for nothing.

Josie's mum said, 'Listen, whatever Eileen's done, it's not your fault, even if she does say it is.'

'I know,' said Josie Smith, 'but she made me put it on so I was wearing it when, when . . . and Eileen's mum never shouts at her but she shouts at me.'

'There'll be no shouting done,' said Josie's mum, 'unless I do it. Painting her coat pink! That's a real Eileen trick that is. What I can't understand is where she got the paint.'

Josie Smith didn't tell. Rawley Baxter didn't tell because he wanted to keep his two pounds. Eileen didn't tell over Rawley Baxter or Josie Smith because she kept screaming so loud that nobody got a chance to ask her. She didn't come to school next day but she wasn't ill. When Josie Smith got home she came round to show them how nice she looked in her red frock with white flowers and real lace and her pretty new pink coat.

A REAL EASTER EGG

Josie Smith woke up feeling excited. It wasn't Christmas morning but it smelled like a special day. Then she remembered.

'It's Easter Sunday, Percy,' she whispered to Percy Panda's big woolly head on the pillow beside her. Light was coming through the thin curtains but there was no noise at all so it must be very early. Josie Smith scrambled out of her warm bed and went to look out of the window. It was morning but the sky wasn't blue. It was pale pearly pink and the roofs and chimneys were very black like at night. Josie Smith got Percy up and showed him. 'I bet we're the only people up in the whole world.'

Josie Smith liked Easter. It's a day for wearing your best clothes when people come for their tea and getting specks of thin Easter egg chocolate on them. *If* you get an Easter egg.

Josie Smith remembered that she wasn't getting an Easter egg. She felt hungry and a bit sad. Then she saw her garden down in its sunny corner in the yard and remembered her red watering can. She wanted to go down and water her seeds but her mum would hear her and shout. It was too early to get up. Josie Smith got back in bed and talked to Percy about her seeds, trying to get back to sleep. Her feet and hands were very cold and she had left the bedclothes turned back when she got up so they were cold, too. Josie Smith got up again. She tucked Percy in and tiptoed across the landing to her mum's bedroom. Her mum's curtains were thick so it was still night in there.

'Mum,' whispered Josie Smith, trying

not to wake her up so much.'

'What's the matter?' asked Josie's mum, opening one eye. 'Are you poorly?'

'I woke up too early,' said Josie Smith, 'and I can't get back to sleep. Can I come in your bed?'

When she climbed in, her mum said, 'What have you been doing? You're frozen.' She pulled her close in the middle of the bed where it was as warm as toast. Josie Smith fell asleep.

When they both woke up again it was really morning. Rays of sunshine peeped between the curtains and somebody down in the street had their front door open and the radio on.

'Happy Easter,' said Josie's mum and she yawned.

'Happy Easter,' said Josie Smith and she yawned, too.

'You're not upset about not having an Easter egg, are you?'

'No,' said Josie Smith with her eyes a

bit shut. 'And, anyway, Mum? I've seen Eileen's Easter egg and it's got pink sugar flowers stuck on the front and she said she's going to give me one if we only play what she wants all day. Only . . .'

'Only what?' asked Josie's mum.

'Only I promised to help Mr Scowcroft feed his hens and Eileen never wants to come.'

'Well, Mr Scowcroft won't mind if you don't go for once. He'll feed his hens by himself like he does when you're at school.'

'I know but I promised because there's a hen that's sitting. She's called Mavis and she sits all day behind the shed and she won't come for her dinner. I feed her some mash from my hand. Mum, what does she sit there all day for? Why doesn't she get fed up?'

'Didn't Mr Scowcroft tell you?'

'I think he did but sometimes I can't understand what he says.'

'And what did he say?'

'He said Mavis was broody and when I asked him what broody was he just went in his shed. And after, he said he'd bought a setting and when I asked him what a setting was he sucked his pipe and said you'll see soon enough and looked at the sky. Then it rained and I came home.'

'Well, you keep feeding Mavis and you'll see for yourself what he means.'

'I'm going to Mr Scowcroft's then,' Josie Smith decided. 'Can I still put my best frock on because it's Easter?'

'No, you can't,' said Josie's mum. 'You'd be bound to get hen mash all down the front of it. You can put it on after. Come on, let's get up. I've got to bake a simnel cake.'

'What's a simnel cake?' asked Josie Smith. 'Does it have icing on it?'

'We have one every year,' said Josie's mum, 'only sometimes your gran makes it. It's got spices and raisins in it and marzipan and icing on top. Don't you remember?'

'I think I do,' said Josie Smith, 'but I don't remember it as much as Christmas cake.'

Even if she didn't remember, Josie Smith was pleased. She liked cake but she liked marzipan better, and icing even better than that. She got dressed as fast as she could and had some tea and some bacon and tomato on toast. Then she put her wellies on and ran next door to rattle Eileen's letter box.

Eileen came out on the doorstep with her new red and white frock on and a piece of Easter egg in her hand.

'Are you coming to Mr Scowcroft's?' Josie Smith asked.

'No, I'm not. You get dirty there and I've got my best frock on.' She didn't say Josie Smith couldn't have a sugar flower. She just went in and shut the door.

Josie Smith ran round the corner and up the street in the sunshine as fast as she could go.

Mr Scowcroft was mixing the hen mash.

'Finished eating chocolate already, have you?'

'No. I haven't got an Easter egg,' Josie Smith said. She shut her eyes in case he asked her if she minded but he didn't, so she opened them again.

'Shall I feed Mavis, Mr Scowcroft?'

'Aye,' said Mr Scowcroft. Then he

sucked on his pipe, pah, pah, pah, and said, 'It'll not be long now.'

'What won't be long, Mr Scowcroft? Is it going to rain?' Josie Smith looked up at the pale blue sky. Mr Scowcroft always knew when it was going to rain. She waited a bit but he didn't say anything else. Josie Smith carried a handful of warm mash to Mavis's hiding place behind the shed. She crouched down. Mavis made a happy little noise in her throat and reached forward with her long neck to eat from Josie Smith's hand.

'I wish you could talk,' said Josie Smith, 'then you could tell me why you keep sitting in this corner instead of coming for your dinner with everybody else.'

81

But Mavis couldn't talk, she could only make little crowing noises and peck at her mash.

She pecked very carefully but Josie Smith closed her hand a bit to stop the mash slipping through her fingers and Mavis pecked her by mistake.

'Ouch!' said Josie Smith and sat back with a bump. Hungry Mavis followed the handful of mash, standing up just a bit to reach. When Josie Smith saw what Mavis had been sitting on all this time she dropped the mash on the ground and ran off round the shed.

'Mr Scowcroft! Mr Scowcroft! Mavis is sitting on some of your eggs and one's a speckled one! I saw!'

Mr Scowcroft took his pipe out of his mouth and said to it, 'That's right. Not be long now. Speckled one's yours for helping. Real Easter egg for you.'

'Thank you, Mr Scowcroft.' She didn't say it's not a real Easter egg. She didn't say she wanted an egg with sugar flowers in a box like Eileen's. She shut her eyes and didn't say it and Mr Scowcroft went in his shed. Josie Smith liked speckled eggs but she wished and

wished she had an Easter egg like Eileen's. She breathed hard, not crying.

Mr Scowcroft came out and gave Josie Smith six eggs wrapped in newspaper.

'Easter eggs for your mother,' he said. 'Fresh for your breakfasts. Make a nice cake. See you come back this afternoon. If you want to be in time for Mavis you'll have to come early. Now, think on.'

'All right, Mr Scowcroft. 'Bye, Mr Scowcroft!' Josie Smith couldn't run home because of the eggs. She walked down the empty street in the sunshine, thinking about everybody eating their Easter eggs.

'Mr Scowcroft sent you these eggs,' she told her mum. 'He said they're Easter eggs but they're only ordinary eggs really.'

'Take those wellingtons off,' said Josie's mum, 'they're covered in hen food.'

A sunbeam was warming the sunny corner out in the yard. The kitchen was warm, too, because the oven was on. The cake was baking and there was a lamb chop and mint sauce for Josie Smith's dinner.

'Can I put my best frock on, now?' she asked.

'No, you can't,' said Josie's mum, 'I don't want you spilling gravy down it. You know what you are.'

Josie Smith, in her kilt and cardigan and with no Easter egg in a box, was fed up. When she was eating her dinner, her mum said, 'What's to do with you?'

'Nothing,' said Josie Smith, squeezing her eyes shut. After dinner she asked, 'Mum? Are we having cake now?'

'No. The cake has to be iced when it's cool. It's for tea when your gran comes. You go out and play. I want five minutes' peace.'

'There's nobody to play with.'

'Play by yourself, then. I want a rest.'

Josie's mum went for a lie down on the couch and Josie Smith went out and sat on the doorstep. She looked up the street and down the street and there was nobody. She looked up at the pale blue sky above the black chimneys and there was nothing. Not even a bird. Not even a cloud. It was very quiet. Josie Smith looked at the doors of all the houses. They were all shut tight. Everybody was inside. Everybody was eating Easter eggs. Josie Smith felt upset. She went and rattled Eileen's letter box. Eileen came to the door with a bit of chocolate on the real lace collar of her new red and white frock.

She looked at Josie Smith and said, 'What have you got your horrible old kilt on for? It's Easter Sunday.'

'Well,' said Josie Smith with her eyes shut, 'I don't care.'

'I've got three Easter eggs,' Eileen said. 'How many have you got?'

Josie Smith was just going to shut her eyes and say Loads, but then she thought Eileen wouldn't give her anything so she said, 'You promised I could have a sugar flower.'

'Well, you can't,' Eileen said, 'because I've eaten them all just now.'

'You promised!' shouted Josie Smith. 'You're my best friend and you promised!'

'I didn't say Cross my Heart and Hope to Die,' Eileen said and she went in and shut the door.

Josie Smith stood in the quiet empty street and her chest squeezed tighter and tighter because she felt lonely and she wanted an Easter egg like everybody else. Then she heard somebody whistling. Right at the bottom end of the street, Jimmy Earnshaw was going past on his two wheeler bike. Josie Smith wanted to marry Jimmy Earnshaw because he gave her Ginger. And sometimes he gave her a ride on his crossbar and that was better than any Easter egg. Josie Smith started running down the street as fast as her wellingtons would go. But she was too shy to shout and Jimmy Earnshaw didn't notice her at all. He rode away past the corner. He was gone. Josie Smith stood still. It was quiet again. She had stopped near Geoffrey Taylor's door. Geoffrey Taylor wasn't as handsome as Jimmy Earnshaw because he had red hair and freckles, but he sometimes helped Josie Smith with her sums and his dad was nice. And his dad always bought Geoffrey Taylor loads of presents and things, to make up for his having no mum. Josie Smith knocked at Geoffrey Taylor's door and Geoffrey Taylor opened it.

'Are you playing?' asked Josie Smith.

'I can't,' Geoffrey Taylor said, 'because me and my dad have eaten four Easter eggs between us and my dad says we have to go for a walk.'

He went in and shut the door.

Josie Smith stood in the empty street and her chest squeezed tighter and tighter because she was lonely and she

87

wanted an Easter egg like everybody else.

Next door to Geoffrey Taylor's was Gary Grimes's house. Josie Smith didn't really like playing with Gary Grimes because he was soft and because he played with stupid little cars all the time but she was fed up of being by herself and he might give her a piece of his Easter egg.

Gary Grimes came to the door wearing slippers with zips up the front and chocolate all over his face.

'Are you playing?' asked Josie Smith.

'No, I'm not,' Gary Grimes said, 'because I've still got two more Easter eggs to eat.' And he went in and shut the door.

Josie Smith stood in the empty street and her chest squeezed tighter and tighter and tighter because she was lonely and sad and she wanted an Easter egg like everybody else.

There was nobody left to call for now except Rawley Baxter and his little sister, but Rawley Baxter never played with anybody. He only played Batman and his sister had to be Robin. Then Josie Smith remembered her doll. She'd left it at Rawley Baxter's the other day when she ran away after he painted Eileen's coat.

Josie Smith didn't want to go in Rawley Baxter's yard. She was frightened of the face that she'd seen looking out of the window and, even though she liked the grey rabbit that lived there, the yard was sad. But she had to take her doll home so she went to the end of the street hopping and singing, 'If you tread on a nick you'll marry a stick and a blackjack'll come to your wedding.' She did that to pretend not to be frightened. Then she went round the corner and up the back to Rawley Baxter's gate.

Rawley Baxter was wearing his Batman mask and ordering his sister about.

'Start the batmobile, Robin,' he said, and his little sister went in the shed.

Josie Smith followed her. The doll was still there in the bed that Rawley Baxter's little sister had made for it with a crate and newspapers.

'I've come to take my doll home,' said Josie Smith. 'Thank you for looking after her.'

Rawley Baxter's little sister stopped starting the Batmobile and started crying. She didn't say anything. She never said anything. She didn't make a noise, either. She just stood there looking up at Josie Smith and great big tears spilled down her cheeks.

'Take no notice,' Rawley Baxter said behind his mask. 'She's fed up because she hasn't got an Easter egg.'

'Why hasn't she?' asked Josie Smith. She thought she was the only person who hadn't got an Easter egg.

'Easter eggs are a ridiculous price,' Batman said. 'My dad bought a tin of toffees we can all share.'

Josie Smith didn't want to say she hadn't got an Easter egg either. She didn't want to be sad like Rawley Baxter's little sister. She wanted to be like Eileen. Rawley Baxter's little sister still stood there looking up at her and tears kept on spilling down her fat cheeks.

'Have you no hanky?' asked Josie

Smith.

Rawley Baxter's little sister wiped her cheeks with her cardigan sleeve and mixed a bit of rabbit food with the tears.

'If you stop crying,' said Josie Smith, 'you can look after my doll for another day.'

Rawley Baxter's little sister stopped crying.

'Start the batmobile,' shouted Rawley Baxter and Josie Smith ran out the gate and up the back towards home. When she got there she ran inside, away from the lonely street, through the house and out into the back yard. There was nobody there. No Eileen  peeping over the wall. No Ginger on the coal place roof. It was empty and quiet. Josie Smith was so sad she was just going to start crying when she saw,

91

in the sunny corner, her garden with its seed packets on sticks and her beautiful red watering can.

'My seeds!' She had forgotten to water them. They were dry and thirsty and all she'd been thinking about was stupid Easter eggs.

She filled her watering can from the tap in the yard and started to give them a drink.

'I'm sorry,' she whispered, 'I didn't mean to forget you. Please don't die!' On her favourite seed packet, Nasturtium *(Whirlybird mixed)* looked sunny and cheerful. Their red, yellow and orange faces smiled at her in their sunny corner. Then something magic happened. The soil that had been dusty and dry and grey, turned black and soft as the water sprinkled it. And in the soft black soil Josie Smith saw something she hadn't been able to see before. There were tiny specks of green everywhere.

'Mum!' shouted Josie Smith, running in with her watering can. 'Mum! Come quick! My seeds are growing!'

Josie's mum woke up and came.

'They really are growing,' she said. 'That's the parsley and there are your antirrhinums.'

'But, Mum, what about nasturtium whirlybird mixed?'

'You sowed those later,' said Josie's mum. 'They'll come up, too, you'll see. Now come on, we've a lot to do before your gran comes.'

'What have we to do?' asked Josie Smith.

'Boil those eggs Mr Scowcroft gave you, for a start.'

'They're not for me, they're for you,' said Josie Smith. 'Are you going to boil them all? What for?'

'Easter eggs,' said Josie's mum. 'Come in and take those wellingtons off and then get your paint box.'

Josie Smith did as she was told. Boiled eggs are not Easter eggs but now her seeds were growing she didn't mind about it. They spread some newspaper out and her mum brought the boiled eggs to the table.

'Mum! They're coloured eggs! They weren't ordinary eggs. Mr Scowcroft gave you coloured eggs for Easter!'

'They were white,' said Josie's mum, 'and I put onion skins in the water to make them coloured. Now you can decorate them any way you want with your paints.'

'And can I put my best frock on?'

'No you can't,' said Josie's mum, 'not if you want to paint.'

'I want to paint,' said Josie Smith. 'I can paint flowers on the front of one egg so it'll be like Eileen's! And a ribbon with a bow!'

'All right,' said Josie's mum, 'and I'm going to paint clouds and birds on mine. And then I'm going to paint one for your gran with you on it.'

'Me?' shouted Josie Smith. 'Me?'

'That's right. With brown eyes and brown hair with a ribbon in it. Won't your gran be surprised?'

'And what about the other eggs? Shall I paint one for my doll? Mum!

Mum! Rawley Baxter's little sister's still got my doll because she was crying.'

'Go and get it back, then. And bring Rawley Baxter's little sister back with you and let her paint an egg. It might cheer her up.'

'Can I put my best frock on to go?'

'No, you can't, not if you want to paint when you get back. Put your coat on, there's a bit of a wind. And bring your gran back with you.'

Josie Smith put her coat on and went out the front door. She ran down the back to Rawley Baxter's and went in the yard. She heard Rawley Baxter and his little sister being Batman and Robin in the shed. Josie Smith looked at the kitchen window but there was no frightening face there. She opened the shed door.

'You have to say "Gee whizz, Batman!"' shouted Rawley Baxter.

'Gee whizz, Batman,' said his little sister very quietly. Then she saw Josie Smith and started crying.

'Don't cry,' said Josie Smith.

'She doesn't want you to take your doll back,' Rawley Baxter said.

Josie's doll was still tucked up in its newspaper bed.

'Aw!' said Josie Smith, 'Don't cry. You can come with her and carry her to our house and you can paint an Easter egg with me. Come on.'

'She won't go without me,' Rawley Baxter said.

Josie Smith put her arm round the fat little sister and said, 'Come on.'

She didn't come on. She was crying but she didn't make a noise. Josie Smith counted up the eggs in her head: one for her mum, one for her gran, one for Rawley Baxter's little sister and one for herself. There would still be two left over.

'You can come, as well, if you want,' she said. So Rawley Baxter came. His little sister carried Josie Smith's doll, holding it very tight.

When they were on their way up the street, Gary Grimes came out on his

doorstep.

'Where are you going?' Gary Grimes asked them.

'We're going to our house to paint eggs,' Josie Smith said.

'Can I come, as well?' Gary Grimes asked.

Josie Smith counted up the eggs in her head: one for her mum, one for her gran, one for Rawley Baxter's little sister, one for Rawley Baxter and one for herself. There would still be one left over.

'I can bring my Easter eggs, if you want,' Gary Grimes said. 'I've still got one and a bit, only, I'm keeping the toy car that was in one. You can have the silver paper. Can I come?'

'All right,' said Josie Smith, 'you can come, if you want.'

So Gary Grimes came.

When they passed Geoffrey Taylor's

house, Geoffrey Taylor came out with his dad.

'We're going for a walk,' Geoffrey Taylor said, 'd'you want to come?' He looked fed up and so did his dad.

'We're going to our house to paint eggs,' said Josie Smith.

'Can we go as well?' Geoffrey Taylor asked his dad. 'Going for a walk's dead boring.'

'If Josie's mum won't mind,' said Geoffrey Taylor's dad, 'We could call and say Hello. And we could take her that box of chocolates and an Easter egg for Josie. You'll be sick if you eat another.'

Josie Smith added up the eggs in her head: one for her mum, one for her gran, one for Rawley Baxter's little sister, one for Rawley Baxter, one for

Gary Grimes and one for herself. She counted them again and when she'd finished adding them up she started dividing them. If she shared her mum's egg, and Geoffrey Taylor shared his with his dad, there'd be enough.

'You can come, if you want,' she said. 'I don't think my mum will mind.'

So they came.

As they walked up the street, Jimmy Earnshaw came round the corner on his bike. Josie Smith held her breath. She liked Jimmy Earnshaw best of all but now she'd given all the eggs away and she couldn't take them back. Sometimes Eileen gave Josie Smith something and then she took it back,

but that was horrible. Jimmy Earnshaw on his bike came nearer and nearer and nearer. Then he rode past them with no hands, whistling. Josie Smith started breathing again. Only Jimmy Earnshaw could ride a real two wheeler with no hands. Josie Smith was glad he hadn't wanted to paint an egg but she wished he had, as well, and she wanted to marry him.

Just when they got to Josie Smith's house, Eileen came out from next door.

'Where are you going?' Eileen said. 'Is it a party?'

'No,' said Josie Smith, 'we're going to paint Easter eggs.'

'You don't paint Easter eggs,' said Eileen. 'They're chocolate. You eat them.'

'These are real eggs,' Josie Smith said, 'from Mr Scowcroft's and they're coloured.'

'They're never!' Eileen said, 'and you're a liar.'

'Now, now, now,' said Geoffrey Taylor's dad, but Eileen just ignored him.

'You're a liar,' Eileen said. 'And, anyway, I had a great big Easter egg with sugar flowers on and a real fluffy chicken inside.'

'I don't care,' said Josie Smith, 'and, anyway . . .'

Josie's mum opened the door. 'Well!' she said looking at Rawley Baxter and Rawley Baxter's little sister and Gary Grimes and Geoffrey Taylor and Geoffrey Taylor's dad standing at the door with Josie Smith. 'Whatever's going on? And, Josie? Where's your gran?'

'I've forgotten her!' said Josie Smith.

Josie Smith ran back down the street for her gran. When she came back with her, everybody else had gone inside and Eileen was still on her doorstep. She was crying.

'What's to do, Eileen?' asked Josie's gran.

'Josie Smith won't let me come to her party and everybody else has come.'

'No!' said Josie's gran. 'That can't be right. You're Josie's best friend. Of  course you can come, can't she, Josie?'

Josie Smith added up the eggs in her head, then she divided them but there weren't enough. She tried to do tens and units with them because when you do tens and units you sometimes carry one. She wasn't very good at tens and units and she had to keep rubbing out the sums in her head and, no matter how hard she tried, there was never an egg left over to carry.

'Can I come?' asked Eileen.

Josie Smith started doing take-aways. If she didn't have an egg herself because she had her seeds and her watering can, Eileen could have hers and Mum could share with Gran and that left one for Geoffrey Taylor to share with his dad and one for Gary Grimes and one for Rawley Baxter and one for Rawley Baxter's little sister.

'All right,' she said to Eileen, 'you can come.'

'That's a good girl,' said her gran, 'but what are you looking so worried about?'

Josie Smith pulled at her gran's arm to make her bend down. Then she whispered, 'Sometimes I get my sums wrong.'

Josie's gran laughed and said, 'Well, you won't be doing any sums today. It's Easter.'

Then they went in.

They all sat round the kitchen table to paint their eggs and there weren't enough chairs so they had to share. People kept saying, 'Don't nudge, you're making me smudge!' And Geoffrey Taylor's dad said it was a

103

poem and everybody laughed.

Eileen didn't know what to paint on her egg so Josie Smith told her. She didn't know how to load her brush with just the right amount of paint, so it didn't dribble, and Josie Smith showed her. She didn't know which colour to use so Josie Smith chose for her. Then Eileen said, 'You have to paint it for me,' and Josie Smith did.

Geoffrey Taylor and Geoffrey Taylor's dad took turns at painting theirs. Josie's mum painted one for Josie's gran. Rawley Baxter painted a Batman mask on his and Josie Smith painted a doll's face on his little sister's. Gary Grimes said, 'I'm going to use every single colour in your paint box,' and he did and smudged them all together.

When they'd finished, Josie's mum said, 'Now we're supposed to eat the eggs for tea with some salad, so if

you all want to stay . . .' She had creases in her forehead and Josie Smith thought she must be doing tens and units with lettuce and tomatoes in her head.

They all said they might as well go home for their tea because they wanted to keep their painted eggs. The creases in Josie's mum's forehead went away. When they'd eaten all the left-over Easter eggs they'd brought and Gary Grimes had been sick, Josie Smith remembered something.

'Mavis! Mum! I've got to go and feed Mavis at Mr Scowcroft's! I promised. And, Mum! He said I had to come early!'

'What for?'

'I don't know, but he said.'

'I bet I know,' said Josie's mum. 'We'll come with you.'

'Good idea,' said Geoffrey Taylor's dad. 'Bit of a walk.'

'But Mum,' whispered Josie Smith, 'Geoffrey Taylor and Gary Grimes might frighten the hens.'

'Don't worry,' said Josie's mum, 'we'll all stay outside the fence.'

So they walked up the street to Mr Scowcroft's allotment. Mr Scowcroft sucked on his pipe and then took it out of his mouth and said to it, 'Just in time.'

'In time for what, Mr Scowcroft?'

'Hatching,' Mr Scowcroft said. Then Josie Smith saw Mavis, scratching and drinking some water from the trough.

'She's not sitting down any more, Mr Scowcroft, so I won't need to feed her after all, will I?'

Mr Scowcroft didn't say anything. He went behind the shed and came back with the speckled egg that he'd promised to Josie Smith. 'Hold it carefully now. Think on.'

Josie Smith held it carefully. Then she looked hard at it.

'There's a hole in it, Mr Scowcroft. I didn't break it . . . It's moving!'

Mr Scowcroft didn't say anything. He sucked on his pipe. Pah. Pah, pah.

The warm egg in Josie Smith's hands was moving. The hole got bigger and a tiny eye looked out and

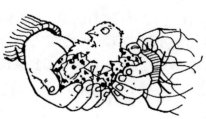

saw Josie Smith.

A beak popped out, then a head. Josie Smith said, 'There's a chicken in it. Mr Scowcroft, what shall I do?'

'Hold it down near the grass,' Mr Scowcroft said.

Josie Smith held her hands with the egg down near the grass. The chick pecked hard and the shell broke in half. The chick looked very wet and a bit worried. It ate some of the eggshell and it kept looking at Josie Smith. Josie Smith looked up to where everybody was watching behind the fence. 'Mum! Look!'

Mavis had gone back behind the shed. Josie Smith carried her chick there and put it under Mavis's wings with its brothers and sisters. They were drying out and looking yellower and fluffier.

'It's your chick that,' Mr Scowcroft said. 'For helping. Come and see it when you want.'

'Can I, Mr Scowcroft? But they all look the same. I won't know it next time.'

'It'll know you,' Mr Scowcroft said.

'You see if it doesn't. Now then. Did you get an Easter egg, or didn't you?'

'I got loads,' said Josie Smith with her eyes wide open. 'Some chocolate ones to share and two real ones to paint for Eileen and Rawley Baxter's little sister and Mavis's speckled egg that was the realest Easter egg of all.'

They all went home for their tea and Josie Smith had two big pieces of cake with marzipan and icing. She went out in the yard to look at her seeds growing three times before bedtime and when she went to bed she had a lot of things to whisper into Percy Panda's woolly ear. She told him about the seeds and the simnel cake and Easter eggs and real Easter eggs and the realest Easter egg of all. She forgot to tell him one thing and that was something she'd forgotten about altogether. She never did get to put her best frock on.